The
Fright-Face
Contest

Other Young Yearling Books You Will Enjoy:

Monsters in the Outfield, *Stephen Mooser*
My Halloween Boyfriend, *Stephen Mooser*
Monster Holiday, *Stephen Mooser*
The Mystery of the Blue Ring, *Patricia Reilly Giff*
The Riddle of the Red Purse, *Patricia Reilly Giff*
The Secret at the Polk Street School, *Patricia Reilly Giff*
The Powder Puff Puzzle, *Patricia Reilly Giff*
The Case of the Cool-Itch Kid, *Patricia Reilly Giff*
Garbage Juice for Breakfast, *Patricia Reilly Giff*
Grumpy Pumpkins, *Judy Delton*

Yearling Books/Young Yearlings/Yearling Classics are designed especially to entertain and enlighten young people. Patricia Reilly Giff, consultant to this series, received the bachelor's degree from Marymount College. She holds the master's degree in history from St. John's University, and a Professional Diploma in Reading from Hofstra University. She was a teacher and reading consultant for many years, and is the author of numerous books for young readers.

For a complete listing of all Yearling titles, write to:
Dell Readers Service, P.O. Box 1045,
South Holland, IL 60473.

The Fright-Face Contest

◆

Stephen Mooser

Illustrated by George Ulrich

A YOUNG YEARLING BOOK

Published by
Dell Publishing
a division of
Bantam Doubleday Dell Publishing Group, Inc.
666 Fifth Avenue
New York, New York 10103

ISBN: 0-440-40242-5

Printed in the United States of America

December 1989

10 9 8 7 6 5 4 3 2 1

W

For
Anastasia and Francis Kralovec

Contents

◆

Chapter 1

◆

The Trog

It was dark and gloomy inside the Creepy Creature clubhouse. Just the way the members of the club liked it. A skeleton and a spider hung from the ceiling. Monster posters covered the walls. In one corner there was an old TV. It was playing a video of *Nightmare Planet.*

Rosa Dorado had just opened a letter. It was from another club. The Monster Card Collector's Club.

"On Saturday they're having a meeting," said Rosa. Her brown eyes sparkled. "It's going to be right here in River City. In Bluebird Park!"

1

Henry Potter was standing next to Rosa. He pointed to a picture at the bottom of the letter. It showed a monster trading card.

"It's a Trog," said Henry. As usual his hair was sticking up in back. Like a feather. "Look at those runny green warts! Get a load of those three bulging eyes! Check out those jagged tusks! Yuck. How gross can you get?"

"It may be gross, but it's the rarest, most valuable monster card anywhere," said Rosa. "And it's the only one we need to finish our collection."

Rosa was in charge of the collection. She had been looking for a Trog for a whole year. She grabbed a strand of her long black hair, put it in her mouth, and chewed. It was a disgusting habit. Her mother told her so. But she couldn't help it. Every time she got excited or worried, she chewed on her hair. And no doubt about it, looking at that card made her excited.

"We have to have it," said Rosa. She held the hair over her lip like a mustache.

"If we get it my monster family will be complete."

"Every year the Card Collector's Club gives away a different card," said Henry. "This year the Trog is first prize in their fright-face contest."

"The rules say anyone can enter. But each person can only enter one picture," said Rosa. "And the picture of the most scared face wins."

Melvin Purdy called out from across the room. Scary things scared him. He didn't want to get near the Trog.

"What's a fright-face contest?" he shouted. His pants were so short you could see his skinny ankles.

"It's a picture of someone being scared," explained Rosa. "Like you. Right now."

"I'm not scared," said Melvin.

Just then a car pulled up outside. Suddenly the engine went *bang*!

Melvin nearly jumped out of his socks.

The members of the Creepy Creature Club laughed.

A moment later there was a knock at the door.

Bam! Bam! Bam! "Open up!"

"What's the secret password?" asked Henry.

Bam! Bam! Bam! "Open up in there!" someone roared back.

Rosa was afraid they might knock down the door to her garage. "Who is it?" she asked.

"Martha Morton! And her son Ollie. Open up!"

"Martha Morton!" said Rosa. "That's Zack's mother. What does she want?"

Zack Morton was head of the Sharks. Zack and the Sharks were the school bullies. The Sharks and the Creepy Creatures didn't like each other. Not one bit. Earlier that year Zack and Henry had even been in a fight. Now they barely spoke.

Rosa opened the door.

"It's about time!" said a big woman in a flowery dress. Her bushy eyebrows were shaped like a V. She stepped into

the clubhouse without being invited. Following behind, like a puppy, was her son Ollie.

Ollie had big ears and a tiny nose. He was wearing a baseball cap, turned around.

Ollie's mom got right to the point. "Zack won't let his brother Ollie join the Sharks. That's too bad. But I can't change his mind. Nevertheless, Oliver needs to be in a club." She looked around the room. "This one will do."

The Creepy Creature clubhouse was filled with scary things. But nothing was as scary as Ollie's mom. Everyone stood silent as stone. And listened.

Martha Morton took Ollie by the wrist. She pulled him forward. "Oliver will make a fine addition to your club. Where does he sign up?"

"But, Mom," said Ollie, "maybe the Creepy Creatures don't want me in their club."

"Nonsense!" said Mrs. Morton. "You're a fine boy! They'd be lucky to get you."

"But—" whined Ollie.

6

Rosa cleared her throat. "Maybe if you came back later we could—"

Mrs. Morton cut off Rosa with a sharp look. "Come back later? Why? We're already here."

"I know," said Rosa. "But if—"

"No buts," she said. "Put him in the club. The boy needs friends."

Ollie's mom looked each club member in the eye. One by one. Then she huffed, spun around, and walked out the door, leaving Ollie behind like a poor abandoned kitten.

Chapter 2

♦

A Kiss for Rosa

It was a long time before anyone spoke. Ollie wiggled his lip with his finger. Everyone stared.

Finally Rosa stuck out her hand.

"Welcome to the clubhouse."

Ollie looked around. Then he shook Rosa's hand. "My mother made me come. If you don't want me in the club I understand."

"How come Zack won't let you be a Shark?" asked Henry.

"I don't think I'm mean enough," said Ollie.

Henry got nose-to-nose with Ollie. He stared into Ollie's blue eyes. "How do we know you're not a spy?"

Ollie looked as if he might cry. He jiggled his lip with his finger.

"Don't be stupid," said Rosa. She put her hand on Ollie's shoulder. "Anyone can see he's not a spy."

Ollie took a deep breath. He looked up at Rosa. "Is it hard to get in your club?"

"Real hard," said Henry. "For one thing you can't be scared of anything. You have to be as brave as Superman." He puffed out his skinny chest. "Like me, for instance."

Everyone laughed. Henry was the world's biggest bragger. No one believed a word he said.

"You have to like scary movies too," said Rosa. "Plus you have to collect monster cards."

"I collect monster cards," said Ollie softly.

"Then someday maybe you can be in our club," said Henry. "Someday. When we have room."

"I understand," said Ollie. He shook his head. "I told my mom you wouldn't let me in."

"We would," said Rosa. "But we can't. Not right this minute."

"No room," said Henry.

Ollie looked down at the ground and sighed loudly. "I guess I'd better be going," he said.

"Sorry," said Rosa. She watched Ollie walk out the door. "See you at school."

After he was gone Rosa said, "Poor guy. I don't think he has any friends."

"I don't think he knows how to make friends," said Henry. "He needs lessons in how to be popular."

"And who would give him those lessons?" asked Rosa.

"How about Mr. Popularity? Me!" said Henry.

Rosa shook her head. "How can Zack be so mean to his brother?"

"Easy," said Melvin. "I fight with my sister all the time."

10

"I wish I had a brother or a sister," said Rosa. "That would be so much fun."

Rosa thought for a moment. She fiddled with her long hair but didn't stick it in her mouth. Everyone watched her in silence. They knew what she was thinking. They all knew how much she wanted someone else in her family. How she dreamed that someday she'd have a little sister or brother to play with.

After a while Rosa looked up and forced a smile. "Okay," she said. "Back to business." She held up the letter. The one with the picture of the Trog. "How are we going to win this contest? We don't even own a camera."

"I have a camera you can use," said Melvin in his squeaky little voice. "I can bring it tomorrow if you want."

Henry laughed. "That camera of yours is worthless. Everything comes out white. Every picture looks like ghosts hunting for a sheet in a snowstorm."

"Then what are we going to do?" whined

Melvin. "Without a camera we can't take a picture. And without a picture we can't win the Trog."

Rosa went to the back of the room and opened a red photo album. It was filled with monster cards. Every one was there. But one. "I have to have the Trog card," she said. "I want my monster family to be complete."

"If anyone can get that card it's me," said Henry. He winked and pointed at Rosa. "For you, my sweet, I'd do anything."

Henry was serious. He liked Rosa.

Rosa rolled her eyes. Sometimes Henry said the silliest things.

Henry blew Rosa a kiss. "Trust me, my little pumpkin. That Trog will soon be yours."

Little pumpkin! Rosa almost gagged. "Win the card for the club, not for me," she said. "Save your kisses for them."

Everyone laughed. Except Henry.

Chapter 3

◆

A Shark in the Milk River

The next day Rosa was sitting in the school cafeteria eating spaghetti, when suddenly . . .

"A snake! Eeeee-yaah!"

Ollie Morton was two tables away, screaming.

"A snake! A slimy snake! On my neck!"

Everyone in the cafeteria froze. Everyone but Zack Morton, Ollie's brother. The school bully was sitting across the table. Sitting next to him was Angie Dobbs. Angie was a member of the Sharks too. She had a turned-up nose and dirty brown hair.

14

Zack had a camera in his hand. He was taking a picture.

"That snake looks dangerous!" yelled Angie. "Don't move!"

"Yikes!" screamed Ollie. His arms were straight up over his head. His little mouth was as round as a wagon wheel. "Eeeee-yaah! Save me!"

"Stay calm!" said Zack. "If he thinks you're afraid he'll bite."

Ollie froze, hands up.

"I'll get him off," said Zack. Reaching across the table, he plucked something off his brother's neck. When he held it up everyone could see it was just a piece of spaghetti.

"Here's your slimy reptile," he said. "Shall we have it stuffed?"

Zack and Angie laughed. Ollie's hands came down. His face was as red as the sauce on the snake.

"You ... you ..." stammered Ollie. "You put that on me."

Zack held up the camera. It was the kind

15

that took instant pictures. "I did you a favor," he said. A picture was sticking out of the bottom of the camera. Zack held it up and watched it develop. "I'm going to enter this photo in the fright-face contest. I'm going to win that Trog card. Little brother, your picture is going to be famous."

Ollie grabbed a little blue bag next to his plate. He held it up to his face and cried. He was so embarrassed.

Zack wrinkled his brow. He didn't realize how much he'd hurt his brother. For a moment he felt bad. Reaching across the table he patted Ollie on the head. "Hey, don't cry. Shape up. Look sharp. Like me and the Sharks."

Rosa shook her head. Sharp! The Sharks were the biggest slobs in school. Zack Morton's flattop had more garbage in it than the city dump. And you could hardly see his freckles for all the dirt.

Ollie pushed Zack's hand away with the bag. He glared at him for the longest time.

16

Then he took a drink of milk and set down the cup. "Leave me alone. Go away."

Zack raised his hands. "Sorry. Hey! What's in the sack?"

Ollie tightened his grip on the bag. "Something for my friends," he said.

"Friends?" said Zack. "I didn't know you had any friends."

"I have lots of them," said Ollie. "More than you'll ever have."

"You don't have any friends," said Angie.

"I do too. The Creepy Creatures are my friends," said Ollie. "I'm going to be in their club."

"The Creepy Creatures!" Zack laughed. He reached for Ollie's bag. "What are you doing with those guys? Those monster lovers are losers."

"Leave my things alone," said Ollie. He grabbed the bag and leapt to his feet. In his hurry, he knocked over his cup.

"Yikes!" screamed Zack. A river of milk flooded across the table. Over the edge it went, like a white waterfall.

17

"My pants!" cried Zack, looking down.

Zack's head came up. His eyes looked ready to explode.

"Why ... why ... you ..." he sputtered, getting to his feet.

Before Zack could do anything, Rosa was standing next to Ollie.

"Leave him alone," she said. "Haven't you heard? Brothers are supposed to be friends."

"Save the mush for breakfast," said Zack.

"Come on, Ollie," said Rosa. "Let's go. Something around here smells."

Zack growled and put his hands on his hips.

"What did you say, creep?"

"You heard me," said Rosa. She took Ollie by the arm. "Come on. Let's go."

"You're not going anywhere," said Zack.

Rosa laughed. "Neither are you. If you walk around looking like that everyone will think you wet your pants."

Zack looked down. He gasped and put his hand over the wet spot on his pants. "Oh, no," he said.

18

Angie giggled.

Quickly Zack grabbed a napkin and tried to wipe off the milk. His face was redder than a vampire's lips. "This is terrible. How can I walk into class with wet pants?"

Rosa and Ollie left Zack muttering to himself. Then they went outside and sat down on the lawn.

"Thank you," said Ollie.

"It was nothing," said Rosa. "Your brother is all talk anyway."

Ollie jiggled his lip with his finger. "I'm sorry I said I was going to be a Creepy Creature. It's just that I don't have any friends and . . ."

"Don't worry," said Rosa. She patted Ollie on the shoulder. "I'll be your friend."

"Really? You mean we can be pals forever?" said Ollie. "Gee, I've never had a friend before. What do I have to do?"

"Being a friend is simple," said Rosa. "There are just five things you have to do."

"Five things?" said Ollie. "Tell me what

they are." He took out a pencil and some paper. "Go ahead. I'll write them down."

"The first thing is that you have to share. Friends share," said Rosa. "The second thing is no lying. Always tell the truth to your friend."

"And the third thing?" asked Ollie, looking up from the paper.

"The third thing is to always stand by your friend. You have to always be there to help her out," said Rosa. "The fourth thing is never tattle on a friend."

"That's easy," said Ollie. "What's the last thing?"

"Don't ever leave your friend with egg on her face," said Rosa. "To me, that's probably the most important rule of all."

"Egg on her face? What do you mean?" asked Ollie.

"Sometimes you get food stuck to your face, right?"

"Yeah, lots of times," said Ollie.

"And it's embarrassing if you go through the day that way," said Rosa. "You want someone to tell you about it so you can wipe it off. A friend isn't afraid to tell."

Ollie held up the paper and read off his list. "Okay. No lying or tattling. You have to help and share. And, finally, you have to tell about food on the face."

"That's it," said Rosa. "Do all that and you'll be my friend."

Ollie beamed. "Pals forever. I'm going to try for it."

"Good," said Rosa. She thought it was fun telling things to Ollie. It was almost as if he were her little brother.

Ollie grinned. He thought that having Rosa as a friend would suit him just fine.

"I brought something for the Creepy Creatures," he said, handing Rosa the little blue bag. "It's from my monster card collection."

Rosa opened the bag. There was a monster card inside.

"Wow!" she said. "It's the Swamp Man. I'd recognize that warty alligator face anywhere. We've got one in our collection, but it's torn."

"It's no big deal," said Ollie. He shrugged his shoulders. "I've got tons of them."

"This is an expensive card," said Rosa. She handed it back. "I can't take it."

"Please," said Ollie. He gave it back. "I want you to be my friend. Take it."

Rosa fiddled with her hair. Nervously, she twisted it between her fingers as she thought about the beautiful Swamp Man card.

"Please," said Ollie. "Friends share. You said so yourself."

Rosa smiled and let go of her hair. "Okay," she said.

Ollie beamed. He'd shared with a friend! He was on his way. Four more things to go and Rosa would be his friend for life.

Rosa couldn't stop looking at the card. "This is the best Swamp Man I've ever seen. You sure you've got more?"

"Oh, yeah," said Ollie. He grinned. "I've got zillions."

Chapter 4

◆

Trouble Knocks

K *nock, knock!*

It was Wednesday afternoon. Someone was banging on the clubhouse door.

"Who's there?" asked Melvin.

"Will," said a deep voice.

"Will who?"

"Will you let in the werewolf?"

"That's the password," said Melvin. He opened the door.

"Yeooow! Yikes!" he screamed. A horrible creature with white bulging eyes was standing in the doorway. Its face was covered with sores. Purple ones.

"Yeooow!" yelled Melvin, covering his eyes.

Pop! Suddenly a flashbulb went off. Melvin opened his eyes. He peeked out from between his fingers. It was Rosa. With one hand she was pulling off a mask. In the other hand was a camera.

"Melvin!" she said. "You covered your face! What's wrong with you?"

"What's wrong with you!" said Melvin. He was still shaking. "You scared me to death."

"That was the whole idea," said Rosa. She held up the camera. "I wanted a picture for the fright-face contest."

Melvin put a hand on his heart. "Do me a favor. Next time pick another face. Please."

Rosa patted Melvin on the shoulder. "I'm sorry," she said. "But you have the best scared face in the club. We have to do whatever it takes to win."

"Hey," said Henry. "Where did you get that camera?"

Rosa smiled. By now all the other club

members were at the door. "I bought it yesterday," she said. She held up the camera. "It's going to win us that Trog card. Everyone who wants to enter can borrow it. The rules said everybody can enter one picture."

Henry looked at the camera. "This must have cost you a fortune."

"Practically," said Rosa. "But nothing is going to stop me from completing my monster family. Nothing."

Just then there was a knock at the door.

"Who's there?" asked Henry.

"Me," snarled someone in a scratchy voice.

"What's the secret password?" said Henry.

"The password is open up or else!"

"That's not the password," said Henry.

"It's Zack Morton. Tell Rosa I want to see her."

Henry stepped up to the door. Before he opened it he turned to Rosa. "Don't worry. I won't let that bully hurt you." He made a fist and snarled. "One punch from me

26

and that big lunk will be on his way to Mars."

Rosa pushed her way past Henry. "I can take care of Zack. He doesn't scare me."

She opened the door.

"I'm glad to see you didn't skip town," said Zack. He had bushy eyebrows and a scrunched-up nose.

"What do you want?" said Rosa.

Zack held out his hand. "Give me back my card. The one with the Swamp Man on it."

Rosa wrinkled her forehead. "That was your brother's card. He gave it to me."

Zack snorted. "My brother doesn't have his own card collection. We share it. He took it without asking."

"He stole it?" asked Melvin.

"More like borrowed it," said Zack. "My little brother has trouble making friends. I guess he thought the card would impress you guys." Zack looked around the room. "Sometimes my brother is a lot like the riddles I like to tell."

27

"How is that?" asked Henry.

"Hard to figure out," said Zack.

Melvin was standing in the shadows. "Rosa, better give him back his card."

Rosa gulped. "I . . . I can't."

Zack's lip curled back. "What do you mean you can't?"

"I . . . I sold it," said Rosa. "At the card shop. In town." She held up the camera. "That's how I got the money for this."

Zack stepped through the door. He poked Rosa in the nose. "I want that card back. Or one that's just as good. Understand?"

Rose pushed away his finger. "You'll get your card."

Zack looked around the clubhouse. "You stole my card. I have a right to take something as payment."

"Don't worry," said Rosa. "I'll get you another one."

"It better be just as good," said Zack. "That card was perfect."

"It will be the same one," said Rosa.

"I want it in time for the card show

28

Saturday," said Zack. He pointed at himself with his thumb. "Did you know I'm going to win a Trog card there? I've already taken lots of scared faces."

"You've been scaring the little kids at school," said Henry. "That's not very nice."

Zack snorted. "Don't be a sore loser."

"We're not going to be losers," said Henry. He pointed to Rosa's camera. "We're going to take some pictures too. We'll scare the socks off those judges."

"Don't make me laugh," said Zack. Now he poked Henry in the nose. "You guys got three days to get my card back. Understand?"

"If Rosa said you'll get it back you will," said Henry.

"I'd better," said Zack. "Or you guys will soon look like my favorite vegetable."

Henry winced. "What vegetable is that?"

Zack pounded a fist into his hand. "A squash," he said. Then he snarled and went out the door.

After Zack was gone Rosa put her head

in her hands. "I can't believe Ollie would do this," she said. "He was supposed to be a friend. Friends aren't supposed to lie. He's going to have to learn the importance of telling the truth."

"Rosa, don't worry," said Henry. "Just call up the card shop. Right now. Tell them you want the card. Then sell the camera and get it back."

"You're right," said Rosa. "That's all I've got to do." Rosa went to the phone and dialed.

She talked to Mr. Dunn at the card shop. Finally she hung up.

"Bad news," she said. "The card's been sold. He just mailed it off."

"Maybe we can get it back," said Henry. "Did he mail it to someone nearby?"

"Nope," said Rosa. "Far away."

"How far?" asked Henry.

"China," said Rosa.

Chapter 5

♦

A Spider for Lunch

On Thursday Rosa got behind Ollie in the cafeteria line.

He had a camera on his plate. It looked like Zack's, the kind that took instant pictures.

Rosa tapped Ollie on the back of one of his big ears. "I want to talk to you."

Ollie turned around. When he saw Rosa his tiny mouth dropped open. "H-h-hello," he stammered. "How are you doing?"

"Terrible," said Rosa. "Thanks to you."

"If it's about the card then I can explain everything," said Ollie. "You see, I—"

"You lied. Lying is one of the worst things you can do," said Rosa. She narrowed her eyes. "Rule number two. Friends don't lie. Remember?"

The line shuffled forward. The smell of hot dogs and sauerkraut filled the air.

"I'm sorry," said Ollie. "I was so excited about sharing, rule number one, that I forgot about rule number two."

"My friends have to obey all the rules. Not just some of them," said Rosa. "That's also a rule."

"I'll study the rules tonight," said Ollie. He sighed. Rosa had just added another rule. He hoped he could remember it. "Give me another chance. Please. I promise I'll learn all the rules. Please. I want to be your friend."

Ollie looked sadder than a dog in a cold rain.

Rosa nodded. "Okay. One more chance. But no more lying, ever."

Ollie's face lit up like a Christmas tree. "Thanks," he said. "I promise. I'll always tell you the truth."

Poor Ollie, thought Rosa. He needs a lot of help. He needs someone who can explain things to him. After a while Rosa realized that what Ollie really needed was an older brother. Someone besides Zack.

"I wish he was my little brother," thought Rosa. "I'd teach him the things he needs to know." She smiled. "I bet I'd be the best big sister anyone ever had."

"Hurry up!" yelled Mrs. Ames, the cook. Everybody was sliding their plate along the counter. As they passed by she spooned out the sauerkraut. *Kerplop! Kerplop! Kerplop!*

"Step lively!" shouted the cook. She waved at Ollie with one of her long, skinny hands. "Move it!"

Ollie reached into his pocket. He put something onto his plate.

Mrs. Ames raised up her spoon, then froze.

"Oh, my!" she gasped. Her free hand flew to her mouth.

The sauerkraut slid off the spoon. The

slimy mess slid down the front of her white uniform. "Eeeee-yaah!" she screamed. "A spider!"

Pop! Ollie snapped off a picture.

Mrs. Ames teetered. For a moment it looked as if she might faint.

"It's just a big hairy fake," said Ollie, grinning. He snatched the spider off the plate and held it up. "See?"

"Why, you little ..." Mrs. Ames exploded. She waved the spoon at Ollie. Bits of sauerkraut went flying. "Why would you scare me like that?"

Now it was Ollie's turn to freeze.

"Speak up!" she roared.

"I ... I needed a picture," sputtered Ollie. "For the Creepy Creatures. For Rosa, because—"

"So this was Rosa's doing!" said Mrs. Ames. She glared at Rosa. "I should have known the Creepy Creatures were at the bottom of this."

Rosa raised a hand. "Mrs. Ames. Please. I—"

"I ought to send you both to the principal's office." She looked down at the sauerkraut still stuck to her uniform. Growling, she flicked off the mess with her hand.

Before she could look up, Ollie and Rosa scooted away. They kept on running. Right through the cafeteria. Out the door. And into the hall.

"There goes lunch," said Rosa, leaning against a locker. She fought to catch her breath. "I hope your picture was worth it."

"I hope so too," said Ollie. He reached down and took the new picture out of the bottom of the camera.

Rosa looked over his shoulder and groaned.

"You didn't aim," she said. "You got a picture of the spoon."

Ollie jiggled his lip with his finger. "And it's not even a scary spoon, is it?"

He crumpled up the picture and put it in his pocket.

"I was going to give you the picture," he said. "So you could win the card." He shook his head. "I wanted to help my friend. That was number three on your list, remember?"

"I also remember what number four was," said Rosa. "Never tell. You tattled to Mrs. Ames. She almost sent me to the principal."

Ollie shook his head. Every time he took a step forward, he took two steps back. At this rate he was never going to be Rosa's friend. He wouldn't qualify in a million years.

"Do you hate me?" he asked.

Rosa shook her head. Were all little brothers this much trouble? she wondered.

Ollie jiggled his lip some more. "Another chance?" he squeaked.

Rosa tapped Ollie on the nose. "All right," she said. "Just remember Rosa's rules of friendship. From now on, follow them."

"I will. I promise," said Ollie. "I'm going to work extra hard so we can be pals forever."

Rosa laughed. "I'm afraid you'll have to work extra extra hard to be pals with Mrs. Ames. She was really mad."

"I guess I scared her pretty good," said Ollie.

"She really freaked," said Rosa. "I've never seen anything like it."

"I have," said Ollie. "Every time Zack sees a bat, even a picture of one, he goes crazy. Crazier than Mrs. Ames."

"He's crazy about the Swamp Man card too," said Rosa. "I think he wants to take something from our club as payment."

"He does," said Ollie. "I know it."

"Really?" said Rosa. "What did he say?"

"He said he's going to do to the Creepy Creatures what the plumber does to the pipes."

"What's that?" said Rosa.

"Clean them out," said Ollie.

Chapter 6

◆

Family Talk

After school Rosa saw Ollie. He was walking along River Street. His cap was turned around. His arms were full of books. His head was down.

"Ollie!" she cried. "Where are you going?"

"Home," he said. He squinted and studied Rosa's face for bits of food. No luck. He couldn't show his friendship today. Her face was as clean as a new bar of soap.

"Do you want to visit the clubhouse?" asked Rosa. She smiled. "We're going to take pictures for the fright-face contest. Our club just has to win."

"Thanks, but I'd better not come by," said Ollie. "I don't think the Creepy Creatures want me hanging around. They're mad at me for getting the club in trouble. They told me so today at school."

"They did?" said Rosa. "Who?"

"I don't want to tattle," said Ollie. "No telling, remember? You said so yourself, rule number four."

Rosa bit her lip. "I'll talk to the Creepy Creatures. Maybe you can come by tomorrow. Would you like that?"

"Sure," said Ollie. "I'd like that. There's never anything to do at my house."

"Don't you ever play with Zack?" asked Rosa.

"He never pays any attention to me," said Ollie.

"I wish I had a little sister," said Rosa. "I'd play with her all the time. And I'd teach her things too."

Ollie smiled. "Like how to make friends?"

"Sure. We'd share secrets and everything," said Rosa.

41

They walked in silence. Along the way they passed other kids. Dan Foote and his brother were in their driveway, skateboarding. The Katona twins were on their lawn, playing catch. Finally they came to Ollie's house. There was a big oak tree in the front yard. A broken swing was hanging from one of the branches. Ollie looked at the swing and sighed.

"Zack acts like I don't even live in the same house," said Ollie. "He never plays with me. Never."

"We're a lot alike, you and me," said Rosa.

"We are?" said Ollie. "How?"

"I'm an only child," said Rosa. "In a way, so are you."

Ollie nodded. He hated to admit it, but Rosa was right.

Chapter 7

◆

The Camera

When Rosa got to the Creepy Creature clubhouse she heard a familiar sound coming from inside: screaming.

"Yikes! Yeow! Eeeee-yaah!"

"Sounds like Melvin Purdy," she said. "What is he afraid of this time?"

Rosa gave the secret knock and went inside. Sure enough, Melvin had been the screamer. He was sitting on the couch, quivering like a jellyfish.

"Oooooh! Stop! That's horrible!"

Henry Potter was nose-to-nose with Melvin. Gleefully, he was telling him a story. Rosa stopped and listened.

"Now imagine this," Henry was saying.

"You're on a tightrope. You're crossing a pit of slimy snakes." Henry wriggled his fingers beneath Melvin's nose. "There's millions of them!"

Melvin squirmed. Rosa noticed that Henry had her camera in the other hand.

"Suddenly, a bat comes flying out of the trees!" Henry picked up a rubber bat from under the couch and threw it at Melvin.

"Yikes!" screeched Melvin.

"You fall into the pit," said Henry. He cackled. "It's horrible! Snakes are crawling all over you. You start to sink!"

"Eeeee-yaah!" screamed Melvin. "I can't stand it. Stop!"

Pop! Henry took a picture of Melvin's twisted face.

"Great!" said Henry. "Together. You and me. We're going to win that Trog for Rosa."

"I hope I live that long," said Melvin, wiping his brow.

"I hope you live longer than this rubber bat," said Henry. He picked the bat up off

45

the floor. "Look, its wing has a tear in it. We'll have to fix it later."

"If you take any more pictures you'll have to fix me too," said Melvin. He wiped his brow again. "Whew! You tell the scariest stories."

Rosa smiled and walked to the back of the room. She took the red album down from a shelf and opened it up on the table. She never tired of thumbing through the monster card collection. Every horrible, twisted, warty face was like a friend. Or a member of her family.

Rosa turned to the last page. There was a blank spot in the middle. It was the place where the Trog belonged. The empty spot reminded her of the empty place in her own house. And in her heart. The place where a brother or sister belonged. She fiddled with her hair and dreamed about a time when both her monster family and her real family would be complete.

Then, all at once, Melvin was screaming again. "No! No!" he yelled. "Henry, stop! I don't want to pretend my mouth is full of ants. Please!"

Pop! Henry snapped off another picture.

Rosa laughed and started to close the album.

Slam! The door flew open.

Rosa looked up and gasped. "Zack! Angie!"

The two Sharks, Zack and Angie, were standing in the open doorway. They had their hands on their hips and dirty looks on their faces. For a moment no one spoke.

Then Zack stepped forward. He pointed at Rosa. "Your time is up. Fork over the card . . . or else!"

When Rosa didn't answer, Zack and Angie marched into the clubhouse like soldiers. They passed Henry, Melvin, and the others as if they didn't exist. *Clomp! Clomp! Clomp!* They marched right up to Rosa.

Zack thrust out his hand. "Fork it over, I said."

Rosa clutched the red album to her chest.

"Well," said Angie, "where's the card?"

48

Rosa held the album tight.

"Come to the meeting tomorrow," she said. "I'll give you the Trog card then. After we win it."

Zack laughed. "You're not winning that card. I am."

"No way," said Henry. He pointed to the camera lying on the couch. "I just took some scary pictures. They're champions." He winked. "Just like me."

"The only thing you're champion at is bragging," said Zack. He turned back to Rosa and reached for the album. "Since you don't have the card I'll just take this."

Rosa gasped and stepped back. "Don't you dare!"

"You stole his card," said Angie. "He can take anything he wants."

"I could always call the police," said Zack.

Rosa thought she might cry. That album was like her family. She couldn't give it up. She wouldn't. She fiddled with her hair. She put the end in her mouth and chewed. She felt like crying.

49

Just as Zack was reaching for the album Henry walked up with the bat.

"Hey!" he said, waving the rubber bat. "Anyone seen the glue?"

Zack gulped. "Wha-what's that?"

"A bat," said Henry. He shoved it under Zack's nose. "Here. Want to see it?"

Zack jumped. He nearly leapt right out of his shoes. "Ba-ba-bats!" he screamed. "I can't stand them!"

Suddenly Rosa remembered what Ollie had said earlier, outside the cafeteria. About how Zack hated bats worse than anything.

"Henry, give Zack the bat," she said. "Maybe he knows how to fix it."

Zack took a long look at the album. He wet his lips with his tongue and looked again at the floppy black bat in Henry's hand.

"Keep that thing away from me," he said.

"Just take a look at it, please," said Rosa. "I bet you're an expert at fixing things."

Henry waved the bat in Zack's face and stepped forward, smiling.

"Keep away, keep away!" said Zack, backing toward the door. "Bats give me the willies." Suddenly he had forgotten all about the album. He waved to Angie. "Come on. Let's get out of here."

"Please don't go," begged Rosa. "Don't you at least want to hold our furry little flyer?"

"Here!" said Henry. "Catch. I'll throw it to you."

"Don't!" cried Zack. He turned around to run but took only one step before he ran smack into the couch. Headfirst, he tumbled over the arm and smashed into the cushion. "Oof!"

A moment later he had picked himself up and was again hurrying for the door.

"Zack," cried Rosa. "What's the big rush?"

At the door Zack paused. Gasping for breath, he took a last look at the clubhouse. "I'm not coming back ever again," he said. "You can keep your bats and the Swamp Man card too. We're even."

Then he shivered one last time and ran out the door.

51

As soon as he was gone the Creepy Creatures cheered.

"I don't think Zack likes bats," said Henry.

"He hates them more than anything," said Rosa. "Ollie told me so." She looked around the room. "Ollie. The one you said couldn't visit the club."

"That's because he lied to you about the card," said Henry. "He got us all into trouble."

"I had a long talk with him. He promised never to do it again," said Rosa. "So I'm giving him a second chance. Wouldn't you do the same for a brother or sister?"

"Sure," said Henry. "But he's not my brother, or yours."

"Yes, but ..." began Rosa. She stopped. Henry was right. Ollie wasn't her brother, even though she wished he was.

Rosa sighed. "He really wants to be our friend. I think we ought to be nicer."

Henry smiled. He didn't want Rosa to be mad at him. "Okay," he said. "I'll be nicer. I promise."

Melvin stuck his head out the door. He wanted to make sure Zack had really left. When his head came back in he said, "He's gone all right. What a relief. That bully said he was never coming back."

Rosa scratched her head. "Why did he say we were even? He didn't get the album. He didn't get the card either. It doesn't make sense."

"Who cares why he said it?" said Henry. "Now, when I win the Trog tomorrow, we can keep it for ourselves."

Rosa shook her head. "Something doesn't fit. Zack was too nice."

"Maybe he's changed," said Henry. He walked over to the couch and started looking around.

"Zack, change? No way," said Rosa.

Henry got down and looked under the couch. "Hey! Has anyone seen the camera?"

No one had.

"I'm sure I left it on the cushion," said Henry. His hands were on his hips. "Did someone pick it up?"

"Oh-oh," said Melvin. "I think someone might have: Zack."

"Zack?" said Henry.

"Remember?" said Melvin. "He fell onto the couch. He could have picked it up then."

"That would explain why he said we were even," said Rosa.

Henry smashed his fist into his hand. "That porcupine head! How rotten can you get? That camera was filled with pictures. Winning ones too." He waved to the Creepy Creatures. "Come on. Let's go get it back."

"Not so fast," said Rosa. She raised a hand. "That camera belongs to Zack as much as it belongs to me. Remember, I bought it with his card."

Henry flopped onto the couch. "Now we'll never get that Trog."

"We can't even enter one picture," whined Melvin.

Rosa sighed and shook her head. "Looks like my monster family was never meant to be together." She sighed again and thought about Ollie. About how no one in the club liked him. "And I guess I was never meant to have a little brother either."

Chapter 8

◆

The Book

On Friday Rosa saw Ollie sitting in the library. He was reading a huge book.

Rosa walked over and put a hand on his shoulder.

"Hi," she said.

Ollie looked up and grinned. He liked seeing Rosa.

"Hi," he said.

"What are you reading?" asked Rosa.

"The dictionary," said Ollie. He pointed to the word "friend." "I'm studying."

Rosa looked over Ollie's shoulder and

read. " 'Friend,' it says. 'A person whom some-one knows well and likes.' "

"It doesn't say anything about food on the face," he said. He squinted up at Rosa and searched for signs of her lunch. There weren't any. Too bad.

"I'm studying hard so we can be pals forever," he said.

"I can tell," said Rosa, smiling.

Suddenly someone came up and slammed shut the dictionary on Ollie's hand.

"Ouch!" said Ollie. He pulled out his hand, then looked up and saw his brother, Zack.

"Shhh!" said the librarian, Ms. Foster. She was standing behind her desk, her hands on her hips.

While Rosa had been talking, Zack's class had filed into the library. They were scattered around the room, looking at books.

"I thought I told you to stay away from the Creepy Creatures," hissed Zack. "They're creeps."

Rosa poked Zack in the chest. She was mad. Real mad.

"What's wrong with you!" she said. She shot a look at Ms. Foster, then turned back to Zack. Her eyes blazed like coals. "Ollie is your brother. You should be nice to him. Not mean."

"Says who?"

"I do," said Rosa. "You're lucky to have a brother." Rosa lowered her eyes. "Some people don't."

"Leave Rosa alone," said Ollie. He smiled as he practiced rule number three, standing up for your friends.

"Leave Rosa alone, leave Rosa alone," said Zack in a loud, sing-songy voice.

"Zack Morton," said Ms. Foster. She pointed across the room. "Aren't you supposed to be looking for a book?"

Zack quickly grabbed a thin red book off the shelf. "I already got one. See?"

He put the book under his arm without looking at it. Then he gave Ms. Foster a little salute.

Ms. Foster put a finger to her lips. "No more talking."

58

Zack smiled and waited till her back was turned. Then he tapped Ollie on the shoulder.

"Do you know why the Creepy Creatures are like germs?" he asked.

"No. Why?" asked Ollie.

"Because they both make me sick!" He slapped his knee. "Pretty funny, huh?"

"Pretty stupid," said Rosa. "Maybe you don't like the Creepy Creatures, but your brother does." She shook a finger in his face. "Brothers aren't supposed to tease each other and fight. They're supposed to be friends. They're supposed to stick up for each other." She put her hand on Ollie's shoulder. "Ollie knows that."

"Rule number three," said Ollie.

Zack sneered. "So when have you ever stood up for me?"

"You've never given me the chance," said Ollie. "But I would if I could."

"Don't make me laugh," said Zack loudly.

"Shhh!" said Ms. Foster. Her finger to her lips, she started across the room.

60

"Oh-oh," said Zack. "Here comes trouble."

Her shoulders down, her eyes focused on Zack, Ms. Foster charged across the library.

Everyone in the library stopped what they were doing. They held their breath. They waited to see what would happen.

"Zack Morton, this is a library," said Ms. Foster, closing in. "It is not a place for yelling and fighting."

"But, Ms. Foster," said Zack. He clutched the book to his chest as if it were armor. "I was just talking to Rosa and Ollie about my book. That's all."

Ms. Foster pulled up a few inches from Zack and glared down at him. In her hair she was wearing a pair of chopsticks. To Zack they looked as if they were aimed right at him. He gulped again.

His class drifted closer, like sharks smelling blood.

"And just exactly what book were you discussing?" asked Ms. Foster.

"Ummm," said Zack. He pulled the book

61

away from his chest and held it out. Ms. Foster read off the title and drew back her head, confused. Zack's class giggled. A few of them even laughed out loud.

Zack turned the book around. His mouth fell open when he saw the title: *Peter Potter's First Book of Potty Training.*

"I ... ummm," muttered Zack. For a moment it looked as if he might faint. His reputation as a tough guy was on the line. He was so embarrassed that his face didn't get red. It got purple! Everyone in his class was laughing. The Katona twins rolled on the floor, holding their sides.

Then, out of the haze, Zack heard a squeaky little voice say, "That's not Zack's book. It's mine."

"Huh?" said Zack. He looked down. It was his brother, Ollie.

"You were helping me learn something," he said. "Isn't that what big brothers do?"

Ollie reached up and took the book. "Thanks, Zack. You were a big help."

"I was?" said Zack.

"Sure," said Ollie. "Without your help I'd be all alone."

Ms. Foster smiled and patted Zack on the shoulder.

"I was all wrong about you," she said. "Go back to helping your little brother. But, please, do it quietly."

Zack let out a giant sigh. His classmates stopped laughing. The Katona twins got up off the floor. Everyone went back to looking for books.

When they were alone again, Zack said, "Thanks. You saved me."

"It was nothing," said Ollie. He felt wonderful. He had helped his brother. And his brother had said thanks!

Zack took another look at the potty book and shuddered. "If you hadn't spoken up they would have laughed me out of the Sharks. I would have been a goner."

"Hey, what are brothers for anyway," said Ollie.

Zack smiled. "I owe you one," he said.

Rosa lowered her eyes. She wished that

Zack owed her one instead. Tomorrow was the big day. The day of the card collector's fair. The day the Trog was being given away. Probably to Zack.

Chapter 9

◆

Finally Friends

Saturday morning.

Bluebird Park was filled with monsters. The Monster Card Collector's Club was having its meeting. Some people in the club had dressed up like their favorite monster cards. The four-armed horned-nose troll was there. Snowcula, the vampire snowman, was sitting on the grass. And Harry the bat, his sharp vampire teeth dripping blood, was under an umbrella selling tomato juice and lumpy red muffins.

"Dracula's breakfast!" he crowed. "Hurry! Hurry! Have a drink of Dracula's blood and

65

a bite of Frankenstein's brains. Hurry! Hurry! It's frightfully delicious."

Henry got a cup of tomato juice. Rosa bought a muffin.

"Enjoy your breakfast," said Harry the bat. He cackled. "Hope it doesn't scare your stomach!"

Rosa and Henry laughed. Then they walked over to some tables to look at the monster cards. Behind the tables were more people in costume. And on the tables themselves were the cards. Tons of them. All kinds. And all for sale.

Henry and Rosa could only look. They couldn't buy. They didn't have enough money. Anyway, the Trog was the only card they wanted. And it wasn't for sale. It was being given away.

They finally found it on a small white table. It was propped up on a stand. Behind it was a sign. The sign said: "First Prize in the Fright-Face Contest."

"What an ugly card," said Henry, pointing. "Scary, but oh-so-beautiful too."

"It hurts to look at it," said Rosa. "There it is. So close, yet so far." She stomped her foot on the ground. "This has got to be the worst day of my life."

"And it's about to get worse," said Henry. He nodded. "Look. Here comes Zack."

Zack Morton was walking across the playground like he owned the place. When he spotted Rosa and Henry his face lit up. "Hello, creeps," he said. "Look what I've got."

Zack held up a picture. It was a scared face. The poor fellow's tongue was sticking out. His eyes were bulging and his hair was standing on end.

"That's the picture I took yesterday of Melvin!" said Henry.

"Can you believe it?" said Zack. "I found it in my new camera."

Rosa stuck out her hand. "Give us that picture."

Smiling, Zack put the picture behind his back. "Sorry, creeps. I'm entering this in the contest."

67

He laughed, then walked over to one of the tables. There he handed the picture to a lady in a big hat. The lady looked at the picture and gasped. Then she put it in a book and wrote something under it.

"He's going to win," said Rosa. She took a bite of her muffin. She chewed and thought. "It's not fair," she mumbled.

Just then Rosa felt someone tugging at her sleeve. She looked down. There was Ollie. He was wearing his cap, turned around. The instant camera was in his hand.

"Hi," he said. "I was ..."

Suddenly, he gasped. Then, smiling, he patted his chin. "Oh, Rosa," he said, wiggling his eyebrows.

"Hi," said Rosa. "I just saw your brother. He's entered the fright-face contest."

"Rosa, Rosa," said Ollie. He winked and pointed at his chin.

"What?" said Rosa.

Ollie cleared his throat. Again he tapped his chin.

Rosa wrinkled her brow. She shook her head, confused.

Ollie rolled his eyes. Then he slapped his chin. Hard. "Get it? Get it!"

"Ah!" said Rosa. Her eyes lit up. Then quickly she flicked a bit of muffin off her chin. "Why, thank you, Ollie." She gave him a big fat wink. "You're a real pal."

Ollie beamed. "I did it!" he said. "I obeyed every one of your rules. I told the truth, shared, didn't tattle, stood up for you, and now I even told you about the food on your face." He puffed out his chest. "Are we friends now?"

Rosa smiled. She had considered Ollie her friend even before he'd spotted the muffin on her chin. He had worked hard to earn her friendship. And he had.

Rosa stuck out her hand. "Shake, pal."

Ollie shook Rosa's hand. Then he took a deep breath and shuffled his feet on the grass. "Does this mean I can be in the club now?"

"I think so," said Rosa. But Henry cleared

his throat and raised his hand. "Maybe we'd better wait a day or two. Some people are still mad about that card."

Ollie dropped his head. Then, suddenly remembering his camera, he raised it up and grinned. "Maybe it's not too late to take a winning picture," he said. "If I won the Trog card, could I be in then?"

"Sure, of course," said Henry. "But . . ."

"But what?" asked Ollie.

Henry took a sip of his juice. "Getting a scary picture is hard. It takes an expert. Someone like me, for instance. Anyway, there's not enough time."

Ollie nodded. Henry was right. The contest was nearly over. He sighed. Maybe he wasn't meant to be in a club. Maybe he wasn't supposed to have friends.

Rosa held out her muffin. "Want a bite?"

"No, thanks," said Ollie. Then, seeing the muffin up close for the first time, he said, "Yuck! Where did that come from?"

"From Harry the bat," said Rosa. She

pointed. "He's over there. He sells tomato juice too."

Henry held up his cup and cackled. "Dracula's blood," he said. "Frightfully delicious."

Ollie looked over at the giant bat. He looked away, then suddenly looked back again. *Blam!* An idea slammed into him like a steel fist. He snapped his fingers. "Harry the bat!"

"The muffins are good," began Rosa. "Get the ones that ..."

But before she could finish her sentence Ollie was gone. Off he dashed, like a cat after a mouse.

"He must be starving," said Henry.

"He's like a little brother to me," said Rosa. She twirled her hair between her fingers. "I hope he gets in the club. He's a good kid."

"He really is," said someone behind Rosa. She turned around. It was Zack. "He saved my neck yesterday. I owe him."

Rosa sighed. She was glad Zack liked

Ollie. Maybe now, at last, they could be like real brothers.

She was thinking about what it would be like if Ollie were her own brother when she was interrupted by the lady in the big hat.

"Attention! Attention!" came her high, squeaky voice over the loudspeaker. "Time to announce the winner of the fright-face contest."

Rosa looked up and gulped. For a moment she thought she might cry. The Trog was about to go to a new home. But it wasn't going to be hers. "Rats," she muttered. "My monster family will never be together now. Never."

Chapter 10

◆

A Bat to the Rescue

Everyone looked up to the front. The woman in the big hat was standing behind the Trog table. She had a microphone in one hand.

Rosa shook her head. "This is the saddest day of my life," she said out loud.

"For me it's the happiest," said Zack. "I'm about to be a prize winner."

Rosa turned around. She was about to say something. But the words never came out. That's because someone behind Zack spoke up first.

"Hey! You, Zack Morton," he said.

Zack turned around. As soon as he saw who had spoken he started to scream. "Eeeee, yikes!" His hands went straight up into the air. "A bat!"

The world's largest bat, a big hairy thing with sharp teeth, was standing right behind Zack. Lifting his black wings, he leaned in close and said, "Boo!"

Zack almost leapt out of his freckles. And the hair on his head nearly blasted off for the moon.

"Eeeee ... yi-yi-yikes!"

Suddenly, there was Ollie with the instant camera. *Pop!* There was a flash of light as he took a picture.

Zack was frozen stiff as a stick. Finally the bat smiled and stuck out his hairy paw. "I don't think we've properly met. I'm Harry the bat. Want some tomato juice? Maybe a muffin?"

Ollie smiled and lowered the camera.

"Thanks, Harry," he said. "You're a real friend."

Harry winked. He flashed his pointed

teeth. "Friends help each other, right? You said so yourself."

"What's going on?" shouted the woman in the big hat. Like everyone else, she had heard the screaming. "Is everything all right?"

Ollie took the instant picture out of the bottom of the camera. He looked at it, then shouted to the lady. "Everything is just fine. Perfect, in fact."

A moment later he was sprinting toward the front, waving the picture over his head. "Gangway! Here comes another scared face!"

While Ollie hurried to the front, Zack slowly snuck a peek at Harry the bat. "Hey! You're not a real bat. You're just dressed up."

"Your brother told me to come over and introduce myself," said Harry. "I didn't know you'd be so scared."

"I hate bats," said Zack. He put his hand on his chest and shut his eyes. "Wow!"

"He scared you pretty good," said Rosa.

Zack shook his head. He took a deep breath. "I guess I had that coming."

"You did?" said Rosa.

"Remember?" said Zack. "Yesterday in the library I told Ollie I owed him one." Zack grinned. "I think he just collected."

Zack searched the crowd. "Where did he go anyway?"

"He's turning in the picture he just took," said Rosa. She pointed up to the front. "See? There he is. Talking to the lady in the big hat."

Everything came to a halt while the lady studied the picture. Then she called over two gray-haired men. They looked at Ollie's picture too. After they'd whispered back and forth, the lady spoke.

"We have a winner."

"I've got a bad feeling about this," said Zack.

Rosa put the end of her hair in her mouth. Nervously, she chewed and waited and watched.

"The winner is . . ."

Rosa crossed her fingers.

". . . Ollie Morton," said the woman. "Ollie, come up and get your Trog."

Ollie leapt into the air. His hat went flying. Then he dashed to the front, like a poked rabbit.

Zack shook his head. "I've got to give Ollie credit," he said. "That kid is just like a new knife."

"A new knife?" said Rosa.

"Yeah," said Zack, proudly. "Real sharp."

Rosa never heard the end of the joke. She was already on her way to the front, weaving her way through the crowd.

"Ollie!" she yelled.

"Rosa!" said Ollie, looking up.

Then all at once they were hugging and spinning around on the grass. They were best friends, laughing out loud.

"You did it! You did it!" said Rosa.

Ollie beamed. He handed the Trog to Rosa. "Here," he said. "Friends share, rule number one."

Rosa stared at the card. Her eyes got a

little misty. She couldn't believe it! She held it to her chest and spun around.

"Now your family is complete," said Ollie.

Rosa put her arm around Ollie's shoulder. "Thanks," she said. She sighed. Ollie Morton had been more than a friend. He had helped her dreams come true.

Just then Henry and Zack came walking up.

"Congratulations," said Henry. "That was a great trick." He stuck out his hand. "Come by the club on Monday. I think we might have a place for you."

"Really?" said Ollie. He shook Henry's hand.

"Maybe there might even be a place for you in the Sharks," said Zack.

Ollie nodded. "I think I'll go into the Creepy Creature Club," he said. "But there is something you're part of that I would like to join."

Zack raised a finger. "Name it."

"Our family," said Ollie. "Will you be a real big brother to me?"

Zack nodded. He reached out a hand

and mussed up his little brother's hair. "I'll try," he said.

Ollie couldn't remember when he'd ever been so happy.

"I'll never forget those rules," he said to Rosa. "Thanks for teaching me how to be a friend."

Rosa sighed. "I think you taught me something too. Something I never realized before about being a friend."

"Not another rule,"said Ollie.

"Sort of," said Rosa.

Ollie shook his head. "Just when I finally learn the five rules of friendship you add another. What is it?"

"The most important rule of all," said Rosa. "It's that real friends don't need rules. They like each other no matter what."

Ollie grinned. "That's the kind of rule I like."

Rosa looked at her card. Her monster family was complete at last.

She put her arm around Ollie and gave him a little hug.

"Pals forever," she said.

Ollie grinned. He had been waiting all his life to hear those words. He hugged Rosa back and said, "Pals forever."

Monster Jokes

Hi! It's Zack Morton again. Did you like the jokes and riddles I told in the story? If you did, here are a few more. As one skeleton said to the other, I hope these tickle your funny bone.

Werewolf Number One: How can you do so many stupid things in one day?
Werewolf Number Two: I get up early.

Which side of the swamp monster has the most warts?
The outside.

What do you call a zombie with a bell?
A dead ringer.

How do you contact a shark?
You drop him a line.

What do you call someone who puts his right arm down a dragon's throat?
Lefty.

Joe: What kind of candy does Dracula like best?
Clerk: All-day suckers.

What are the worst kinds of ants to have at a picnic?
Gi-ants.

Monster: Waiter, I can't eat this food. Call the manager.
Waiter: Forget it. He won't eat it either.

What did Dracula take for his sore throat?
A coffin drop.

What do you call a giant vampire?
A big pain in the neck.